Chores Chores Chores!

Salina Yoon

PSS!
PRICE STERN SLOAN

every room, room, room!

I hate to wipe, wipe, wipe.

I need a break, break, break!

I hate to fold, fold, fold.
It's getting old, old, old!

I hate to brush, brush, brush, brush in a rush, rush, rush!

I hate to fluff, fluff, fluff. It makes me huff, huff, huff!

My Chore Chart

CHORE LIST	♡	♡	♡
Dust	⭐	⭐	⭐
Vacuum	⭐	⭐	⭐
Windows	⭐	⭐	⭐
Rake leaves	⭐	⭐	⭐
Fold laundry	⭐	⭐	⭐
Dry dishes	⭐	⭐	⭐
Brush Harry	⭐	⭐	⭐
Fluff pillows	⭐	⭐	

I hate chores! But when I'm done, done, done...

PRICE STERN SLOAN
Published by the Penguin Group
Penguin Group (USA) Inc., 375 Hudson Street, New York, New York 10014, USA
Penguin Group (Canada), 90 Eglinton Avenue East, Suite 700,
Toronto, Ontario M4P 2Y3, Canada
(a division of Pearson Penguin Canada Inc.)
Penguin Books Ltd., 80 Strand, London WC2R 0RL, England
Penguin Group Ireland, 25 St. Stephen's Green, Dublin 2, Ireland
(a division of Penguin Books Ltd.)
Penguin Group (Australia), 250 Camberwell Road, Camberwell, Victoria 3124, Australia
(a division of Pearson Australia Group Pty. Ltd.)
Penguin Books India Pvt. Ltd., 11 Community Centre,
Panchsheel Park, New Delhi—110 017, India
Penguin Group (NZ), 67 Apollo Drive, Rosedale, North Shore 0632, New Zealand
(a division of Pearson New Zealand Ltd.)
Penguin Books (South Africa) (Pty.) Ltd., 24 Sturdee Avenue,
Rosebank, Johannesburg 2196, South Africa

Penguin Books Ltd., Registered Offices: 80 Strand, London WC2R 0RL, England

ISBN 978-0-8431-3202-1   10 9 8 7 6 5 4 3 2 1